Hush-a-bye Babies

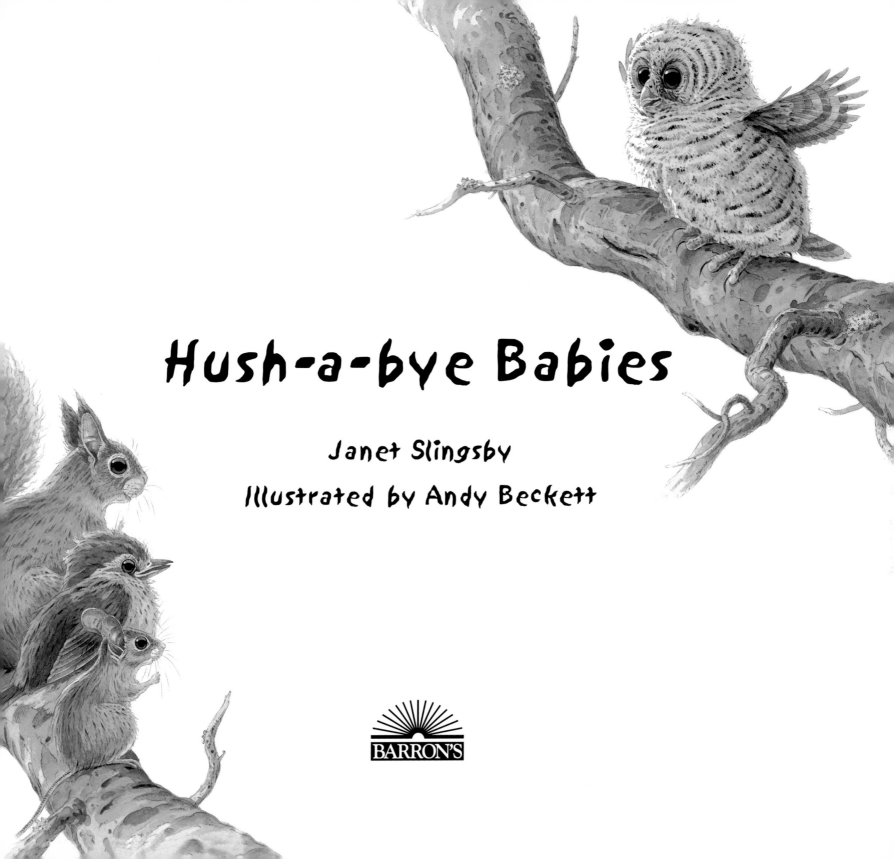

Hush-a-bye Babies

Janet Slingsby

Illustrated by Andy Beckett

BARRON'S

The wood was still and quiet. It was the end of the day—time for the sun to leave the sky and for baby animals to go to bed.

In the big tree, Mother Bird was softly singing her babies to sleep.

"Squawk! Screech!
Scream and t-wit-a-witta-woo!"

Someone was making a horrible noise!
Mother Bird flew down the tree
to see who it was.

Hop, skip, and jump,
one baby bird, who was only
pretending to be asleep, hopped
out of the nest and followed her.

"Please be quiet," said Mother Bird to the noisy creature. "You will wake up my babies." But the strange animal just squawked more loudly.

"Why," said Mother Bird, looking more closely at the fluffy feathers, "you are just a baby. I'll try to sing you to sleep."

So Mother Bird tried singing her most tuneful song
but this baby showed no signs of falling asleep.
It just got noisier!

The squirrel family at the top
of the tree heard the commotion.

"The children will all wake up if that noise
continues!" said Papa Squirrel.

"Let's go and find out what's happening,"
said Mama Squirrel.
They ran down the tree.

Hop, skip, and jump, one baby squirrel,
who was only pretending to be asleep,
skipped out of the nest and followed them.

The squirrels and Mother Bird
looked at the noisy baby. "I've tried
singing a lullaby," said Mother Bird,
"but that only seemed to make it noisier!"

"Our babies are rocked to sleep by the wind
in the branches," said Mama Squirrel.
"Let's make the branch sway, and perhaps we'll
rock it to sleep," suggested Papa Squirrel.

Mother Bird hurriedly flew up
to watch from a safer perch.

"That certainly didn't work,"
said Mama Squirrel, catching
her breath. "It thinks we
are playing a game!"

"T-wit-a-witta-woo!" giggled the strange baby.

In the roots of the tree, Daddy Mouse heard the strange noises. He looked to see that his babies were all asleep and ran up the tree to see what was going on.

Hop, skip, and jump, one baby mouse, who was only pretending to be asleep, jumped out of the nest and followed him.

Mother bird and the squirrels told
Daddy Mouse about the noisy baby.

"We always cuddle our babies to sleep,"
said Daddy Mouse.

So Mother Bird and the squirrels tried to cuddle
the noisy baby. Perhaps the strange creature was
ticklish because it laughed and laughed.

"Squawk! Screech! Scream and t-wit-a-witta-woo!"
it cried, louder than ever.

The noise was so loud that the rabbit family heard it in their burrow under the ground. Mr. and Mrs. Rabbit came out to see what was going on. Daddy Mouse, Mother Bird, and the squirrels hurried down to tell them about the noisy baby.

As soon as all the grown-ups were gone, the baby bird, the baby squirrel, and the baby mouse began to chatter together.

"Let's go and talk to it!" said the little squirrel.
"It's got feathers and it looks like a sort of bird to me."

"I'm not scared," said the little bird.

"Let's hold hands," said the little mouse.

So, holding tight to each other, the three little animals crept along the branch towards the noisy baby.

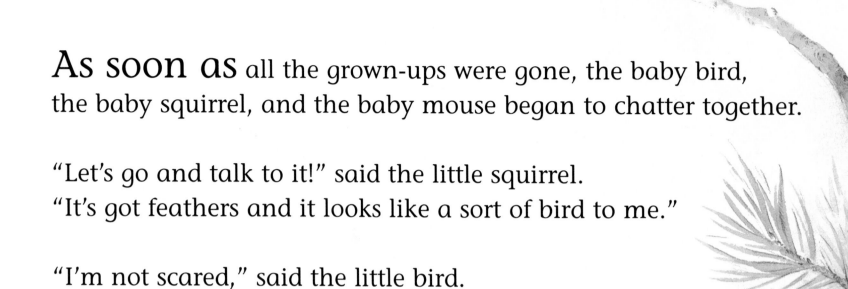

"Hello," said the little squirrel.

"Hello," said the little bird.

"Hello," said the little mouse. "Why are you making such a noise? It's bedtime!"

"It's not my bedtime,"
said the noisy baby.

"I'm an owl and I'm waiting
for my Mommy. We go out at
night and sleep during the day."

"**I wish** I could stay up all night!"
said the baby squirrel.
"Me too!" squeaked the baby bird.
Baby mouse tried to agree but was stopped by a big yawn.

"Shush," said the little owl suddenly. They all listened hard.
They heard a faint swish-swish of big wings in the distance.

"That's my Mommy!" cried the baby owl.
"Sounds a bit scary," said the little squirrel.
"It's very dark out here," said the little bird.
"I'm tired, I want my Daddy!"
said the little mouse.

"I'm going home," said the little bird. He flew up
to his nest and snuggled down with his brothers and sisters.
In no time at all he was fast asleep.

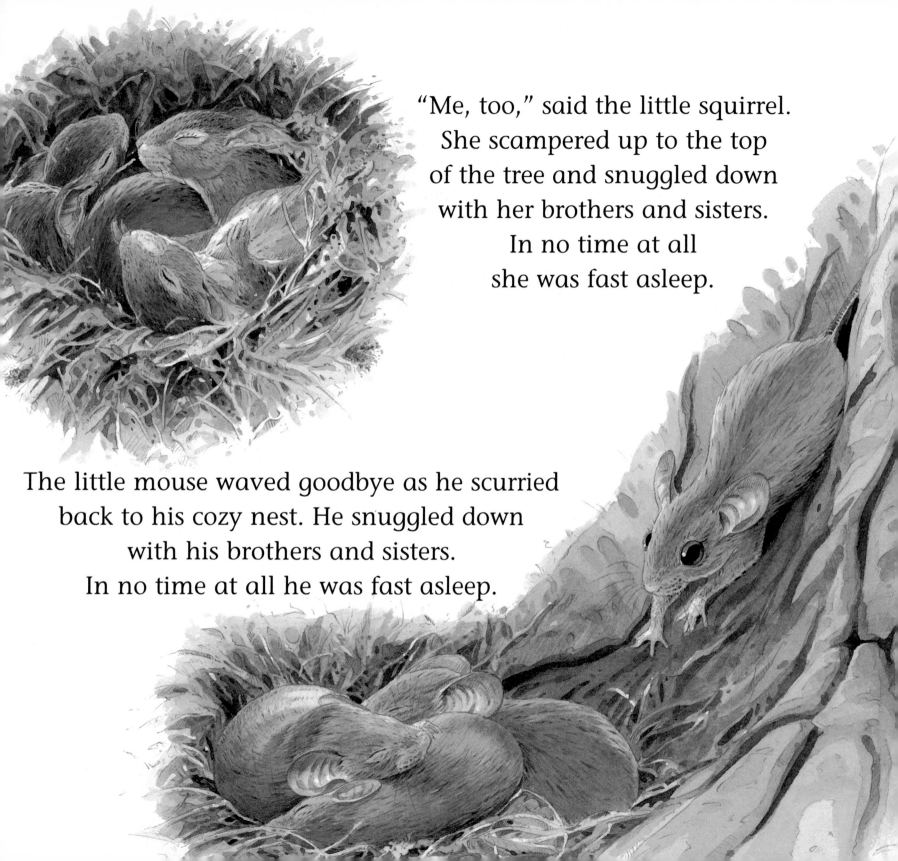

"Me, too," said the little squirrel.
She scampered up to the top
of the tree and snuggled down
with her brothers and sisters.
In no time at all
she was fast asleep.

The little mouse waved goodbye as he scurried
back to his cozy nest. He snuggled down
with his brothers and sisters.
In no time at all he was fast asleep.

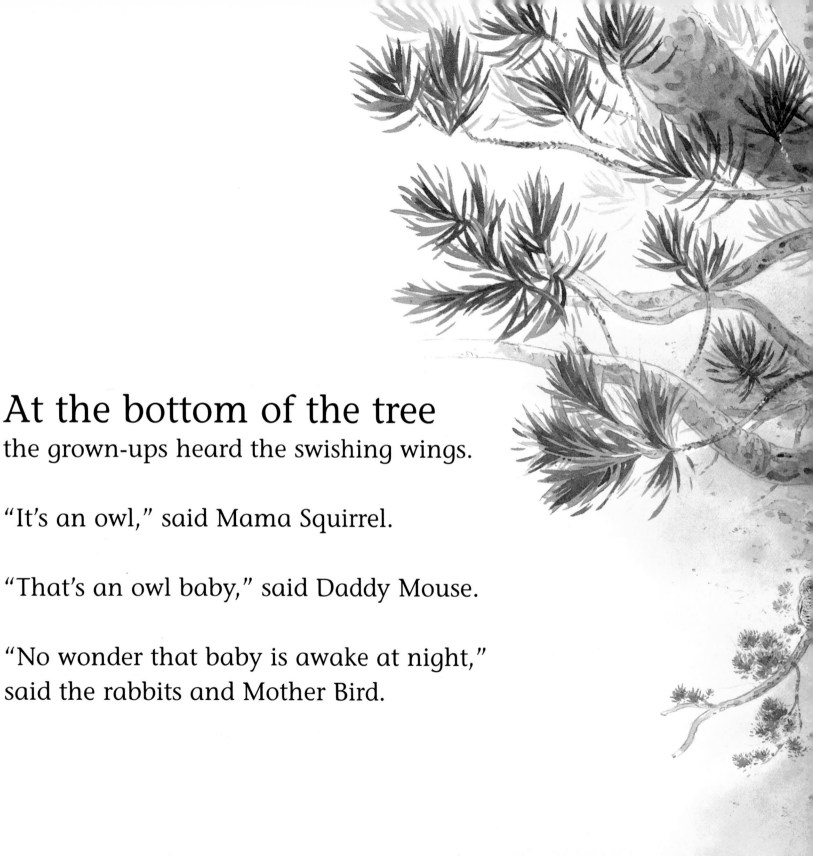

At the bottom of the tree
the grown-ups heard the swishing wings.

"It's an owl," said Mama Squirrel.

"That's an owl baby," said Daddy Mouse.

"No wonder that baby is awake at night,"
said the rabbits and Mother Bird.

The mother owl hugged her owl baby.
"I hope you've been good while I've been away,"
she said.

The baby owl giggled and gave
a very little screech.

The owls flew off into the night and Mother Bird, the squirrels, Daddy Mouse, and the rabbits hurried back to find all their babies fast asleep in their cozy nests.